FANG

For HOWARD,
who is brave and has
a fiercely fine way with words.
(B.S. Hazen)

To my wife, JUDITH, and my
daughter, MELISSA.
(L.H. Morrill)

FANG

by Barbara Shook Hazen

*illustrations by
Leslie Holt Morrill*

Atheneum   New York

I have a dog. His name is Fang.
He is big and fierce-looking.
That's why I picked him.

I picked him so he could protect me
from all the things I'm scared of, like
the big bulldog next door,

and the big kids on the corner,

and the big waves at the beach,

and the big thunder booms when there's
a bad storm and, most of all,

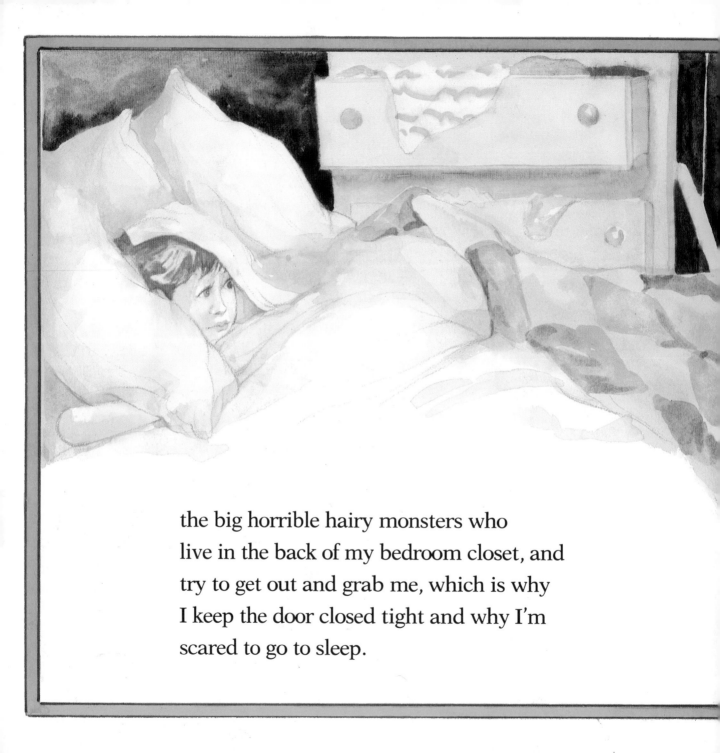

the big horrible hairy monsters who
live in the back of my bedroom closet, and
try to get out and grab me, which is why
I keep the door closed tight and why I'm
scared to go to sleep.

The only trouble is, Fang is not fierce. He is big, but he is not brave. He is afraid of more things than I am. He is afraid of things that aren't even scary,

like little puppies,
and little babies,
and little bath-water waves.

He is so afraid, he is even afraid of himself,

which is why I always talk to Fang
in a soft voice, because I am the one thing
Fang isn't afraid of.

I try to help Fang be less afraid.
I tell him, "Look, it's just a little
puppy. It wants to play."

I tell him babies can't bite, they don't
even have teeth yet, and bath-water waves never
hurt anybody. I tell him, "That's YOU
in the mirror."

Then I hug him, and tell him I love him
anyway, even if he is a big coward,
instead of big and brave.

But sometimes that doesn't work. So I try pretending I am big and brave, just to show Fang. I hold my breath and walk by the big bulldog next door.

Then I walk right by the big kids.

At the beach, I leap into the water
and don't even think about the waves.

When there's a thunderstorm, I stay on top of the bed.

And when I want to pretend I am really
brave, I take a deep breath and close
my eyes tight and yank open the closet
door and yell at the top of my lungs,

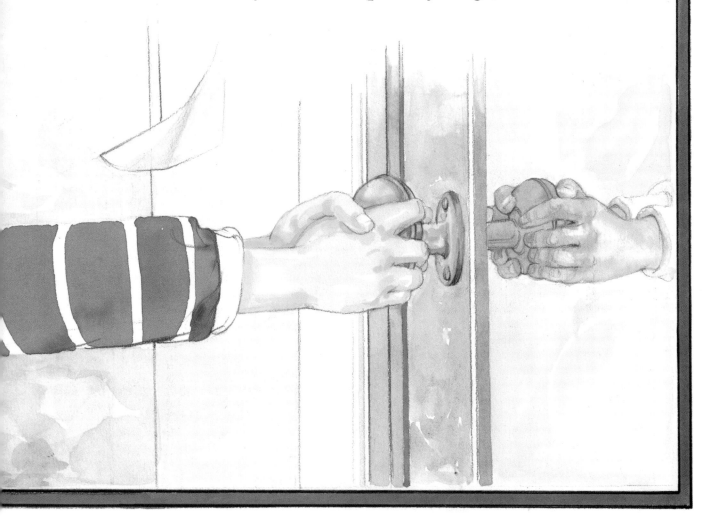

"SEE FANG, THERE AREN'T ANY MONSTERS INSIDE!"

Then I feel something hairy. I hear
something crash. I open my eyes,
expecting the worst, and know what?

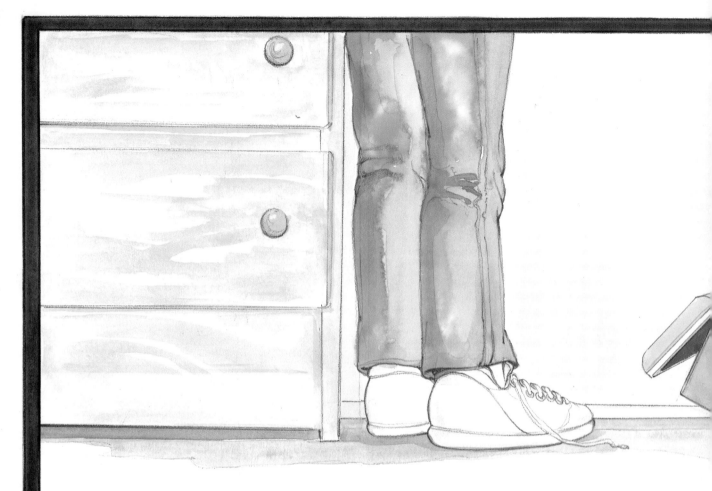

There aren't any monsters any more.
There is only Fang, scrunched and scared,
in the back of the closet, under a lot of
boots and Christmas ornaments and boxes and
my old baby stuff.

I am so happy I hug Fang and tell him.
"Good dog. We did it. We chased those
monsters away. There's nothing to be
scared of now." And there isn't either!

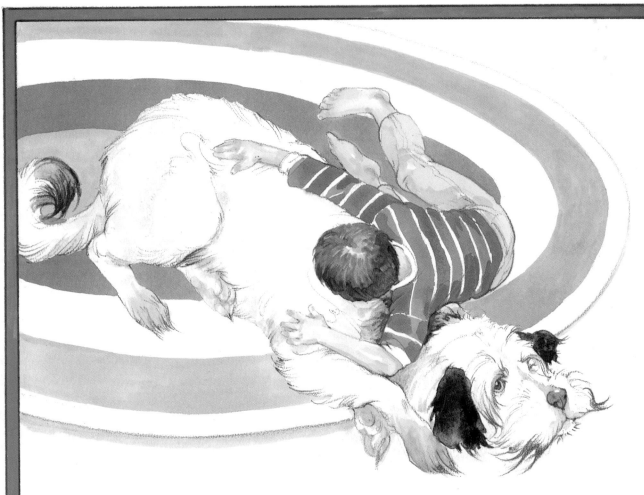

Text copyright © 1987 by Barbara Shook Hazen
Illustrations copyright © 1987 by Leslie Holt Morrill

Atheneum. Macmillan Publishing Company. 866 Third Avenue, New York, NY 10022
Type set by Fisher Composition, New York City. Printed and bound by Toppan Printing Company, Japan.
Typography by Mary Ahern. First Edition.   10 9 8 7 6 5 4 3 2

Library of Congress Cataloging-in-Publication Data

Hazen, Barbara Shook.   Fang.   SUMMARY: Although he is big and looks fierce, Fang the dog is afraid
of so many things that he is even afraid of himself. [1. Dogs—Fiction.   2. Fear—Fiction]
I. Morrill, Leslie H., ill.   II. Title.   PZ7.H31497Fan   1987   [E]   86-28697.   ISBN 0-689-31307-1

E   Hazen, Barbara Shook
HAZ
         Fang

$13.95

BAKER & TAYLOR BOOKS